W9-CEB-313

Praise for *A Distant Father*

"It is amazing how, in so few words, Skármeta is brilliantly able to paint the soul's complexities and turn the world into a less uncertain place. With exquisite prose, as faint as a sigh, Skármeta weaves a fun and ironic story of the tortuous road toward maturity."

—**FÉLIX J. PALMA**, author of the *New York Times* best seller *The Map of Time*

"In this spare, but emotionally rich and big-hearted new novella *A Distant Father*, the prize-winning Chilean author Antonio Skármeta accomplishes his usual magic of rendering with profound dignity the dilemmas of the human heart. Jacques, a young schoolteacher in the small village of Contulmo is on the cusp of a defining moment, a crisis of identity and manhood that unfolds in a masterfully told story. Desire confronts Jacques with life choices that present a clash of values: to stay with his beloved mother in their rustic idyll; to reunite with his abandoning Parisian father and pursue a more cosmopolitan life; or to explore a passionate relationship with the lovely Teresa. A poetic soul who finds beauty in the ordinary—winter apples, spiders building webs in a corner—

Jacques's haunting journey is archetypal
and one we all share: becoming a Self.
Written with exquisite calligraphic precision,
A Distant Father is a book that plunges the reader
into longing and loss, possibility and hope,
and never strays from the heart's truths."

—**DALE M. KUSHNER**, author of *The Conditions of Love*

"Each fragrant line of *A Distant Father*
is in just the right place. Without excess,
every word is positioned with the precision
of an artist who works with his eyes closed, fluidly.
Without artifice, without sterile rhetoric,
and without pyrotechnics."

—*La Vanguardia*

"This charming little book possesses
an amazing storyline, many love stories, and it has,
at the end, an extraordinary surprise."

—*Frankfurter Allgemeine Zeitung*

A DISTANT FATHER

ALSO BY ANTONIO SKÁRMETA

The Days of the Rainbow

The Dancer and the Thief

The Postman (Il Postino)

A Distant Father

ANTONIO SKÁRMETA

TRANSLATED
FROM THE SPANISH
BY JOHN CULLEN

OTHER PRESS
NEW YORK

First published as *Un padre de película*
by Editorial Planeta, Barcelona, Spain, in 2010.

Production Editor: Yvonne E. Cárdenas
Text Designer: Julie Fry
Typeset in Clarendon and Palatino

10 9 8 7 6 5 4 3 2 1

 Printed in the United States of America on acid-free paper. For information write to Other Press LLC, 2 Park Avenue, 24th Floor, New York, NY 10016. Or visit our Web site: www.otherpress.com

Library of Congress Cataloging-In-Publication Data
Skármeta, Antonio.
[Padre de película. English]
A distant father / by Antonio Skármeta ; translated from the Spanish by John Cullen.
pages cm
ISBN 978-1-59051-625-6 (pbk.) — ISBN 978-1-59051-626-3 (e-book)
1. Fathers and sons—Fiction. 2. Latin America—Fiction. 3. Chile—Fiction. I. Cullen, John, 1942– II. Title.
PQ8098.29.K3P3313 2014
863'.64—dc23

2013044646

A DISTANT FATHER

ONE

I'm the village schoolmaster. I live near the mill. Sometimes the wind covers my face with flour.

I've got long legs, and nights of insomnia have stamped dark rings under my eyes.

My life is made up of rustic elements, rural things: the dying wail of the local train, winter apples, the moisture on lemons touched by early morning frost, the patient spider in a shadowy corner of my room, the breeze that moves my curtains.

During the day, my mother washes enormous sheets, and in the evening we drink lemon balm tea and listen to radio plays until the signal gets lost among the dozens of Argentine stations that crowd the dial at night.

TWO

My village, Contulmo, is smaller than the neighboring town of Traiguén. Before going to the capital to get my teaching degree, I finished high school in Angol, a town much larger than Traiguén. While I was there, I was diagnosed with acute anemia, which the doctors treated by prescribing Scott's Emulsion and injecting bracing shots of cod liver oil into my arms.

A nurse in the hospital initiated me into the vice of smoking cheap cigarettes, and in order to support this habit—which wound up giving me bronchitis—I've had to find a second job.

The work is very modest and very infrequent. Once a week, a truck comes to pick up the sheets my mother washes for the hotel in Angol, and I consign to the driver some translations of French poems that the editor of the Angol newspaper publishes in the Sunday supplement.

My dad is French. He went back to Paris a year ago, when I returned to Contulmo after completing my studies at the teachers' college.

I got off the train and he climbed on.

He kissed my cheeks desperately. My mother was on the platform too, dressed in mourning. My return home has never compensated for my father's absence. He used to sing French songs—"J'attendrais," "Les feuilles mortes," and "C'est si bon."

And besides, he knew how to bake loaves of crispy bread, baguettes, that were different from the local buns and soft breads. He also used to bring lemons and oranges to the market. Every day he'd pass by the mill to get some flour, and that was how he and the owner became friends. When Dad left, I wasn't able to reproduce his skill in baking baguettes, but I've carried on his friendship with the miller.

He knows more about Dad than I do myself.

He knows more about Dad than my own mother does.

THREE

When Dad went away, my mother was suddenly extinguished, like a candle blown out by a gust of frosty wind.

Like her, I loved my father to the point of madness. And I too wanted him to love me back. But he was gone a lot. When he was home, he'd write letters at night on my old Remington portable typewriter and pile them up on the desk for me to hand on when the truck came to pick up the sheets. They were letters to his friends, he said. *"Mes vieux copains."*

Occasionally, when we've been drinking brandy, the miller drops some nugget of information, and so I always listen to him with great attention. But his trails lead nowhere. He keeps things quiet by talking about them. Or rather, he talks about things *while keeping them quiet.* It's as though he had a secret pact with my father. *Un jurement de sang.*

When Pierre decided to leave, I was just about to graduate from the teachers' college in Santiago. The week before I was to arrive in Contulmo, elementary school teaching certificate in hand, he told my mother that the cold climate of southern Chile cracked his bones, and that a ship was waiting for him in the harbor at Valparaíso.

I got off the train and he got on, boarding the very same car.

In southern Chile, the trains still belch smoke.

My father shouldn't have left the same night I arrived. I didn't even get a chance to open my suitcase and show him my diploma. My mother and I wept, both of us.

FOUR

The texts I translate are simple. Things the people around here can understand. Poems by René Guy Cadou. Village verses, not cathedrals of words. By contrast, the Santiago press publishes monumental poems, verses chiseled in marble, rich with allusions to ancient Greece and Rome and meditations upon the eternity of beauty. In Santiago, *El Mercurio* prints such poems and accompanies them with illustrations of Paris and Rome. Below the text, in parentheses, the translator's name appears.

Here in the provinces, beauty is never eternal.

Sometimes I include an original poem of my own in the envelope with my translations and ask the editor to consider publishing it. His response, though negative, is courteous, given that he never rejects my poems and never prints them either.

FIVE

The first month of Dad's absence nearly killed my mother. She's never gotten over it completely. She's merely convalescing. When I got a teaching post at Gabriela Mistral Elementary School, she livened up a little. There was even a trace of joy in her approval, because my new job meant I wouldn't abandon the village like the Mapuche kids who left and wound up kneading dough in Santiago bakeries.

We got no letters from Dad. Which didn't mean he hadn't sent any. The thing is, mailmen don't come to these villages, and asking the truck driver to inquire in the Angol post office whether there was any mail for her would have wounded my mother's pride.

It really rains a lot here; I constantly have a cold. On a normal day, I teach children literature and history, and after school I harvest potatoes, lemons, and oranges, depending on the season.

Now and again, I fill a few baskets with apples and bring back flour from the mill. Cristián is an assiduous drinker of red wine, and his apron is eternally spattered with purplish stains. He always offers me a glass, which however I always decline. Drinking alcohol makes me sad.

Although I'm almost always sad, wine makes me sad in a different way. It's as if a very deep solitude were entering my veins.

Ever since Dad went away, I want to die.

SIX

I devote most of my time to smoking and sharpening my Faber No. 2 pencils. I use them to correct my pupils' compositions, and if there's something I don't like, I rub it out with the eraser on the pencil's other end and suggest a better phrase.

The Remington's actually a loan from the mayor, who let me have it so that I could make fair copies of my translations.

The children's compositions are quite optimistic. Most of them begin by saying something like, "The day opens with the sun, which spreads its kind fingers over the field," or "When the cock crows, dawn breaks and the shadows put on yellow robes."

Only Augusto Gutiérrez stands outside the norm. For example, he writes, "The sun's crowing bursts the cock's eardrums."

In math he's a disaster. He's repeating the previous year, and he's the only boy in the class with a hint of mustache on his upper lip.

He has two sisters. On Sundays I go to the village square, buy some candied peanuts and a Bilz soda, and sit on a stone bench. When the sisters pass close to the bench, they burst into mocking laughter and I turn red.

Augusto Gutiérrez has thick eyeglasses and thin lips. He'll be fifteen next Friday. He walks through the square carrying a volume by Rubén Dario. He knows by heart "The sea is lovely, Margarita, and a subtle scent of orange blossoms rides upon the breeze," but he's not so much interested in the Nicaraguan poet's verses as he is in carrying on a man-to-man conversation with me.

He wants to know, he declares, if I've been to the whorehouse in Angol and how much it costs to spend a night there with one of the girls.

I brush crushed peanuts off my blue trousers and say that such a conversation between a pupil and a teacher is improper. He says that if I don't want to tell him about life, he'll ask advice from the priest in the confessional.

He adds that his birthday party next Friday will offer more than just cake and candles; there's also going to be romantic North American music that people can dance and make out to. His sisters asked him to invite me. Teresa's seventeen and Elena's nineteen.

I'm twenty-one. Everybody around here is very respectable, and I have no doubt that Teresa and Elena come from a good family, but every time they go to Santiago, they buy dresses with plunging necklines and tight jeans that cling to their hips and squeeze the air out of my lungs.

SEVEN

Tonight I went to bed without eating and was rude to my mother. I'm irritated because I've never been to the whorehouse in Angol, just to the hospital there. It angers me that I had nothing to tell Gutiérrez. I too would like to know the girls' prices.

I'm listening to the radio, a special broadcast with Lucho Gatica y Los Peregrinos. A bolero called "Amor, amor, qué malo eres"—"Love, love, you're so wicked"—is all the rage, and the band plays it three times. Fans calling in to Radio Sureña have voted it the tune of the week. I like the part that goes, "Proud towers that once stood so tall collapse in humiliation." Those words speak to my heart. Someday, the little Gutiérrez sisters who make sarcastic faces at me will collapse in the mud, and I'll watch them from on high.

EIGHT

Even though it's night already and I still have to prepare my Monday classes—in history, I'm supposed to cover a very big topic, namely the Spanish Civil War and the murder of Federico García Lorca—I get up from the rough sheets that Mama washes until they're immaculate and that the climate dampens and chills until they make me shiver.

I head for the mill.

Cristián pretends not to be surprised to see me and asks if I've got any cigarettes. I offer him one and in return he uncorks a bottle of red wine. He fills two milk glasses that measure a quarter of a liter each and instructs me to drink mine down in one gulp. When the glasses are empty, I feel like a rocket exploring the darkness of space.

According to the miller, we're heroes, he and I. The simple fact that we haven't left the village is epic.

"I give the children bread, you give them education," he tells me, spitting a few tobacco grains onto his apron. "The world's not made for small villages. But our presence makes them big. One of these days, some high government official will give us a decoration. There'll be a pavilion in the square with your name on it. Your father was a cosmopolitan man, a Parisian—he must have really loved you if he was willing to bury himself in this place for five years. We spent many hours playing cards together."

"Have you ever been to the whorehouse in Angol, Cristián?" I fire the question at him impetuously, drunkenly, stupidly.

He fills his glass with wine. I cover mine like a coffin so he won't pour me any more.

With a gesture that's supposed to be majestic, I get to my feet and look up at the starry sky. My mind's spinning faster and higher than the cosmos.

"Tomorrow's Saturday, Jacques. You're not teaching any classes, I'm not baking any bread. The train to Angol leaves at noon. But the action doesn't start until after dark."

"Doesn't matter," I say from under a hail of meteorites. "If we go during the day, I'll have time to buy a birthday present for Gutiérrez."

"The sisters' little brother?"

"He's having a birthday party next Friday. His sisters look at me and laugh when we're in the square."

"The younger one has the hots for you."

"For me? How can that be, Cristián?"

"They both have a thing for Frenchmen."

"But I'm a Chilean, and a poor one at that."

"But you're young. You have a profession, you haven't settled for milking cows. Someday the education ministry will send you to Angol. Or even to Santiago."

"It worries me to hear you say that."

"Why?"

"If we go with whores today and then I get a teaching position in some other school and someone declares he's seen me in the whorehouse, what happens to my academic career?"

"The principal of the high school visits the girls, too."

"Don't give me that!"

"Whatever you do, there'll always be someone trying to impose limits on you. Don't go looking for them on your own. What are you going to give Gutiérrez?"

"A pair of boxing gloves. I saw him shadow-boxing on the basketball court."

"He's fifteen years old and he's already getting a mustache."

"He takes after his father. Have you heard anything from my dad?"

"Not a thing, kid."

"You said that funny. Is he dead?"

"He's not dead."

"Well, you say you haven't heard from him, so how do you know he's not dead?"

Cristián pours himself another glass of wine, emptying the bottle.

I lie down on the floor.

"What's wrong with you, buddy?"

"I'm drunk."

"That's all right. But there's no need to get all dramatic. What's bothering you?"

"Gutiérrez's sister."

"The younger one or the older one?"

"The younger one, Cristián. Those tits she's got, they make me want to squeeze them until they pop like grapes. Her teeth gleam in the night. I imagine myself biting her lips, and then she touches me..."

"How?"

I don't want to answer. I'm standing in the universe, vertical and alone. I'm a dog beaten by moonlight. Why did my father leave us?

"The younger Gutiérrez girl's a good choice. The older one..."

"What about her, Cristián? What about the older one?"

"She's very mature. She could cause you problems."

"What sort of problems?"

"I'm gonna get another bottle."

"Answer my question first."

"Strange things go on in that girl's life. Do you remember when she went away on vacation in January and didn't come back until August?"

"What are you saying?"

"Nothing. I just find it strange, that's all."

"I left the village, too. I went to college in Santiago."

"Right, you were gone two years. She was gone nine months."

"And during that time the younger one used to go walking around the square with a fireman, hanging on his arm."

"And then, all at once, both sisters took to wearing less clothing. It was as if they weren't from here anymore. Didn't you ever notice?"

"That girl drives me crazy. If I go to the party on Friday and dance with her, I'll probably tell her I love her."

Cristián takes two cigarettes from my pack and puts one in my mouth. We light them from the same match.

"Our trip to Angol will help you avoid doing that."

"Anyway, I don't have much money. I can barely afford cigarettes."

"I'll pay for the girls. You can reimburse me later."

"All right, Cristián. I'll buy the train tickets."

I gaze up at the moon. I feel like rolling on the ground.

NINE

The following day, we're in the train station. The station clock is stopped at ten minutes after three. According to my watch, it's almost noon.

Cristián appears, carrying a small, coffee-colored case, like the kind people who sell aspirin use. He's wearing a beige jacket, and he's so closely shaven no one would ever take him for the miller. His red-veined eyes reveal the only evidence of last night's heavy drinking.

I've put on one of Dad's jackets. It used to be a bit too big for me, but the years seem to have shrunk it. The little silk label sewn into the lining reads GATH Y CHAVES, SANTIAGO.

Precisely because my destination is the whorehouse in Angol, I want to look as though I'm going to the city for "work-related reasons."

And so I've brought along a book by Raymond Queneau that the editor of the newspaper wants to publish in installments. Prose is easier than poetry, but I do get all caught up in the fates of the characters. Maybe that's because so little happens here. We're secondary figures, not protagonists.

As the train comes rolling in, whistling and huffing smoke, Augusto Gutiérrez appears on the platform. A toothbrush and a tube of Kolynos toothpaste are sticking out of the lapel pocket of his school jacket.

"Are you going to Angol?" he asks.

"Yes," I reply, blushing hot and red all of a sudden.

"What for?"

"The movie theater's showing a film about Paris. I want to see it because I'm translating this book."

I show him *Zazie dans le métro.*

"What's the name of the movie?"

"*Quai des Brumes,*" I say, inventive but disciplined.

"You're lying."

"No I'm not."

"Will you be back for my party?"

"Of course. I plan to buy your present this very afternoon."

The train stops in the station. The stationmaster looks up at the Roman numerals of the clock, whose hands always point to ten after three, and passes a cheese sandwich to the engineer. As usual, nobody gets either on or off.

But the painful images come back: I'm returning

home, I get off the train, Dad gets on the train, the train leaves.

"I'm afraid they might close down this line," the stationmaster tells us. "Railroad's streamlining, and this stretch isn't profitable. I hate to think about being out of a job at my age."

"What time's the train leave?"

"In a couple of minutes. My wife's fixing a thermos of coffee for the engineer. We make a little extra income with things like that. Incidentally, I've also got fresh homemade Chilean éclairs, a hundred pesos each. You interested?"

"When we come back."

Augusto Gutiérrez pulls at my sleeve and makes me lean toward him; my forehead bangs against the hard frames of his spectacles.

"Please take me with you to Angol."

"We can't do that, kid."

"Why not?"

"It's a secret."

"You're going to the whorehouse."

"No we're not. I'm going to buy you a present. I don't want you to see it before Friday."

"As long as it's not a globe. You already gave me a globe last year."

"You didn't like it?"

"What can I say? All those countries, right there in front of me, and I'm stuck in this pit."

He gestures toward the cow that's crossing the tracks.

"How am I any different from her?"

"You're different because you know what you want and you have self-awareness. The cow's always just a cow. She's not even aware she's a cow. She's all cow, all the time. But you, on the other hand—your awareness makes you free."

Gutiérrez takes off his glasses and reveals his eyes, the soft, sad, watery eyes of the myopic. He says, "I'm going to be fifteen years old, Prof. I don't want to feel humiliated next Friday because I'm not a real man yet."

"You're a child, Gutiérrez. We'll talk about it when you turn sixteen."

"I'm going to be dead by the time I'm sixteen. You'll recognize my grave because a mound will rise up over it. The same mound that forms under my sheets every night."

The miller grabs the boy by one ear and pulls him several meters in the direction of the street. "Go on home, you annoying little brat!"

While he's trying to get out of Cristián's grip, the boy shouts to me, "Professor, sir, take me with you to the whores!"

I climb into the car so I won't have to see him anymore. But he breaks away from the miller and comes to my window. "I'll fix you up with my sister," he says, panting. "She's crazy about you."

"The younger one or the older one?"

"The younger one. She wrote you a letter."

"How do you know?"

"She keeps it in her dresser. With her bras and panties."

"What does the letter say?"

"You have a distinguished air."

"What else?"

"You're a cultured man."

"Me?"

"She looks at my globe and says she'd like to be lying on the beach at Acapulco with you."

"Acapulco? How did she come up with that?"

"She listens to that song on the radio, 'Remember Acalpulco, María Bonita.' She's out of her mind for sappy boleros."

"What else does the letter say?"

"Other things."

"Tell me."

"If you take me to the whorehouse."

I give him a tap on the forehead. "I can't, Gutiérrez. I'm your teacher, not your pimp."

The train starts to move. Before climbing aboard, the miller aims a blow at the kid, but he dodges it with catlike agility.

A pair of boxing gloves is a good idea, I think with a sigh.

Just as the train leaves Contulmo, I see my pupil on the platform cup his hands around his mouth like a megaphone. "Do one for me, Jacques!" he shouts.

He means I should climb on top of one of the girls and dedicate the ensuing bonk to him.

TEN

In the little fishing harbor near Angol, we lunch on fried hake and Chilean salad. I remove the onions from my tomatoes, picky eater that I am.

Cristián drinks half a liter of white wine and then accepts the fisherman's offer of a siesta on his boat. The miller covers himself with sacks and a net and asks me to wake him up before it gets dark.

When the girls are open for business.

We have to show up early, because demand is very high on weekends.

I go into town and start looking in shop windows. I see articles of clothing made by local artisans, things like scarves, caps, heavy woolen socks. A chess set whose pieces are Japanese samurai, advancing sword in hand. A professional-quality soccer ball autographed by Leonel Sánchez. A Mexican parrot made of thin silver sheets. A Bavarian clock with two dancing boys in leather pants. A photograph of Marlon Brando in *The Wild One,* sitting on a motorcycle with an unlit cigar between his lips. A deck of cards whose backs are all reproductions of *Playboy* centerfolds.

And I also see some splendid red leather boxing gloves.

Just about all the items I see are beyond my means, except for an album bound in blue velvet with an inscription in gold letters: *Diary of My Life.* I ask the shopkeeper to gift-wrap it and buy two packs of Richmond cigarettes with the change. I find a shady spot on the corner, lean against a fire hydrant, and have a smoke.

I open Raymond Queneau's book and use a red pencil to mark the words I'll have to look up later in my *Larousse français–espagnol.*

ELEVEN

In the course of an hour, I notice that the little town I'm in moves about as slowly as a watch, and I try to think up some possible conversational gambits to use on the girls. Nothing particularly witty comes to mind; it even occurs to me that Gutiérrez would handle the situation better than I could. I've been with girls before, but never in a bed. Classmates, girls from the neighborhood.

There's nothing less conducive to wit than being a schoolteacher in the provinces. I walk over to the movie theater, a few steps away. At seven this afternoon, they're showing *Rio Bravo,* starring John Wayne, Dean Martin, and Ricky Nelson. The coming attraction for next week is *Wild Is the Wind,* with Anna Magnani. In a still photograph, John Wayne, wearing a sheriff's badge on his lapel, is looking at Angie Dickinson's bare shoulder; Angie's got on a short petticoat with black lace insets, and the seams of her stockings go all the way up to her buttocks.

"Rio Bravo is a film about becoming a man," the advertisement says. Maybe that's why I keep staring at the photograph for so long, and at the one beside it, too: Ricky Nelson, in a crouch, holding a pistol whose barrel disgorges a tremendous amount of smoke.

A few passersby pause briefly in front of the posters and then continue on their way, except for a man with a black wool cap. He pushes a baby carriage, stops to light a cigarette, and glances without interest at the publicity stills. At first I can't see his face, but he stands there smoking for so long that I end up recognizing him just as he throws away his cigarette end, turns, and crushes it under one shoe.

On the point of losing my balance, I clutch desperately at the baby carriage.

"Dad?" I say.

The man peers confusedly into the little carriage and only then looks up at me. Those are his thick brows, his slightly hooked nose, his bottomless, moist, hidden eyes, and most of all, that's his cheek, marked with his old bar-fight scar.

"Jacques? C'est vraiment toi?"

"Of course it's me, Dad."

He looks in all directions, like a cornered thief. He seems to want to make sure he's not dreaming.

"What are you doing here, buddy?"

"I came to buy a gift for a student."

I feel an immense urge to throw my arms around him and inhale the scent of his skin, which smells like a leather saddle.

"Are you with your mother?"

"No, Dad, I'm not."

He pretends to dab at a smudge on his forehead, but in reality he deftly wipes away the troublesome liquid flowing from his eyes. Then he pulls me close and squeezes me in a hard embrace. I don't know why, but I want that embrace to never stop.

When we let each other go, we simultaneously take out cigarettes, but my father is quicker with his lighter and lights us both. He removes a speck from his cheek and looks at John Wayne's picture again.

"*Rio Bravo.* For the past two months, we've been running it as the Saturday matinee."

"What do you mean, '*we've* been running it,' Dad?"

"I work here. *Rio Bravo*'s a very popular movie. A lot of drinking goes on in this town, and people enjoy watching a lush like Dean Martin find redemption and become a good shot again to boot."

"How many times have you seen it?"

"Twelve, fifteen. Depends on this little character here."

He indicates the baby in the carriage. I look at the

child, and Dad takes off its pint-sized canvas cap, meant to protect it from the no-show sun. The baby looks horribly familiar.

"I think I know that face, Pierre."

Dad swallows saliva for a while, as if oppressed by my silence. He looks extraordinarily young. He's my father, but he could also be a friend. Like the miller.

"He's your brother."

"This baby?"

"Emilio."

"Like Zola.

"Voilà. Comme Émile Zola."

"But he's…he's not a real *brother* brother."

"Listen, Jacques, I came here and settled into the darkest corner of Angol. In a dump, in a cave. I have no more life, I wander in the shadows. I never imagined anyone would find me here. I never thought I'd run into my son in this miserable goddamned hellhole."

"What are you doing here, Dad?"

"Going down the drain."

He puts the little cap back on the baby's head and scratches his own scarred cheek. The scar's inflamed again, as though reacting to some kind of allergy.

"Who's the mother?" I ask, quite naturally, but on the verge of fainting, weeping, or dying.

I don't know how to go into certain details.

Pierre gives a deep sigh and uses the butt of his cigarette, which he's never stopped sucking on, to light another one. He forgets to offer me the pack. He also forgets that I'm talking to him. He looks at the sky over Angol; nothing new there. Robust, inconstant clouds. The downpour could start this very moment or an hour from now.

"Daddy?"

"Don't call me that."

"All right, Pierre."

"The word you used is infinitely treacherous."

"I always called you Daddy before you betrayed us."

"I'm the traitor? Me?"

On a foolish impulse, he snatches up the baby from its carriage, squeezes the little bundle very tightly in his arms, and presses his unshaven cheek to the child's lips. He sticks his cigarette in my mouth and pauses to look at a still shot of Dean Martin. I breathe the smoke in deeply and blow it out far from the baby.

"So you never went to France, Pierre?"

"*Jamais.*"

"You've been in Angol the whole time?"

"Yes. Angol, *le petit Paris.*"

"Why didn't you go?"

"Because I wanted to be near you. And your mother."

"You never wrote."

"I declared myself officially dead."

"The miller knew about you. Just last night he told me you were still alive."

"He must have been drunk."

"We were both drunk."

The clock in the square strikes six. My father checks his watch, and a kind of peace settles over him.

"I love this kid."

"As much as me?"

"As much as you, Jacques."

"Then one day you're going to betray him."

"It wasn't betrayal."

"Then what was it, Daddy?"

He spreads his arms in a small gesture, almost as if to defend himself.

"Bewilderment."

"At your age?"

"At my age. I'm not giving you an explanation. I never thought I'd run into you again one day, or into anybody else I'd have to give an explanation to."

"The miller."

"Cristián's a mirror. I stand in front of him, and he's me. You stand in front of him, and he's you. He offers no resistance. But you—you're hard, Jacques."

"It's too late for me, Father. I'm talking about my brother."

He rocks the child in his arms and places his lips on its left ear, warming it with his breath.

"I cover him up too much. The thing is, he spends a lot of time in the projection room, and it's terribly damp in there. If you heard him breathe, you'd say he had bronchitis."

"The projection room?"

"Like I said, I work in this movie theater."

I hand him what's left of the cigarette and press my fingers against my eyelids to calm the conjunctivitis that's devouring my eyes.

"You're the projectionist?"

"It's a dark, solitary place. No one would have ever found me there. I never thought my own son would come spying on me one day."

He grabs his nose and squeezes it until it turns red.

"Even though I once went to Contulmo and spied on you."

"When?"

"I don't remember. Sometimes I dream about traveling to Contulmo and spying on you and your mother. I don't know when I really went or when I just dreamed about going."

He puts Emilio back in the baby carriage and takes two pieces of cardboard out of his peacoat.

"Here are two free passes to the movie theater. You

can use them for today's matinee, *Rio Bravo,* or for the one with Anthony Quinn next Saturday."

I take the tickets and put them in my jacket. "That's nice, Dad."

"Will you bring a girlfriend?"

"Of course, Pierre."

"I'll be on the lookout for you."

He bites his wrist, but I still manage to hear his groan.

"Mama?"

"She's doing well."

"*Well* well?"

"Tolerably well. Like me, Dad. More or less well. We're both more or less tolerably well."

"Do you like teaching?"

"Literature and history, yes. The other subjects bore me."

I'd forgotten his habit of rubbing his hands together and then horribly cracking his knuckles.

"This meeting of ours, Jacques..."

"...is a private matter."

"You're a smart boy. I'm asking you to keep this secret for your own sake, for me, for your mother."

"For Emilio's mother."

Pierre raises his eyes skyward as if he'd like to ascertain precisely which cloud will discharge the first drop of the coming storm. With positively maternal ferocity, he deploys the hood of the carriage over its passenger. I hear the baby's breathing, a sort of clipped snort, for the first time.

"So how's your French these days?"

"Fine, Dad. At the moment I'm translating *Zazie dans le métro.*"

"Don't know it."

"Raymond Queneau."

"Never heard of him. Well, look, now you know where to find me."

"Right."

"If you have the time, come and see *Rio Bravo.* Bring a girlfriend."

"*Au revoir,* Dad."

"*Au revoir, mon fils.*"

TWELVE

The first shades of evening are just falling when Cristián and I enter the whorehouse. Most of the girls are drinking tea or listening to a radio game show where the contestants can win money if they guess the exact price of certain products. One of the girls comes up to me and plants a kiss on each of my cheeks. She asks my name and occupation. "Jacques," I say, and "teacher." Embarrassed, I ask her what she does.

"I'm a whore," she says with a smile.

We go up to her room. She has Indian features, like most of the girls in this part of the country. In Frutillar, they say, there's a whorehouse with girls from German families. This girl has markedly aboriginal bangs, prominent cheekbones, and a carefree smile. She's young and strong. Maybe in a few years she'll be fat, but not now. A teakettle's boiling on the portable cooker in her room, and beside it are two cups containing little bags of Lipton's. The Chilote blanket on her bed is as tough as an animal skin.

"A cup of tea?"

"Sure. Thanks."

While she stirs the bags in the boiling water, she looks at my shoes and then my tie.

"You could start taking off your things."

She comes over to me, loosens my tie, and when my neck appears, kisses me on it, leaving a damp trace behind. Without bending over, I slip out of my shoes and push them under the bed. I always do that, because they're Dad's moccasins. He passed them on to me when I went off to the teachers' college, and they're a little too big.

"It's cold," I say.

"No it's not, baby. It's your nerves."

"I'm nervous?"

"Drink that."

I sip at the cup, just about certain that the liquid's going to burn my tongue. The girl, on the other hand, takes a teaspoonful and blows on the tea before drinking it.

"So what do you teach, Professor?"

"A little of everything. But I prefer literature and history."

"Not geography?"

"Geography too."

"I'm crazy about geography," she declares, blowing

on her tea and sipping it noisily. "I know countries and capitals. I say their names and imagine what they're like."

"Bolivia?"

"That's easy. La Paz."

"Spain?"

"Piece of cake. Madrid."

"Czechoslovakia."

The girl chews a fingernail. She looks at the ceiling and the rug. Then she goes to the curtain, presses her forehead against the windowpane, and gazes out at the street for a while.

"I don't know."

With a professional movement, she throws off her robe, comes up to me naked, and touches me. Now she's deadly serious. She pushes me onto the bed and takes off my clothes. Then she straddles me, bucks her hips three or four times, and I'm off.

"You still have to pay for the whole hour, you know that?"

"No problem."

"Was it good?"

"Sure."

She lifts the bedspread and drapes it over her head like a hood. Suddenly an immense smile spreads over her face.

"Ask me another question."

"Hard or easy?"

"Easy."

"France."

"Paris."

"Très bien," I say, feeling some of my semen ooze out of her and spread over my stomach.

"Do you speak French?"

"Pretty well. My father's from Paris."

"Do you ever see him?"

"No, right now he's in France."

I take her by the shoulders, pull her close to my face, and kiss her on the mouth. I feel like I'm participating in a dialogue for the first time. Until this moment, I've done nothing but obey her orders.

"Say something in French."

"Hard or easy?"

"Hard and long. You have to pay for the whole hour anyway."

"All right. A few lines of poetry?"

"Let's hear them."

I remain quiet a moment to be sure I've got the verses complete in my memory before sending them out over my tongue. There's a fish-shaped spot on the ceiling.

Ah! pauvre père! aurais-tu jamais deviné quel amour
tu as mis en moi?
Et combien j'aime à travers toi toutes les choses de
la terre?
Quel étonnement serait le tien si tu pouvais me voir
maintenant
À genoux dans le lit boueux de la journée
Raclant le sol de mes deux mains
Comme les chercheurs de beauté!

The girl gets off me and walks over to the washstand. She uses a damp cloth to clean her belly and her thighs.

"I didn't understand a thing," she says. "I don't understand anything when I go to the movies, either. The problem is I never manage to read the subtitles. They go by very fast."

"It's a poem dedicated to the poet's father."

"Did you write it?"

"No, but I translated it. You can find it in the *Diario de Angol*'s weekend supplement."

"What does it say?"

"'Ah, my poor father, have you ever guessed how much love you planted in me and how I love, through you, all the things of the earth?' It was written by René Guy Cadou."

"Do you wish you wrote it?"

"I couldn't write a poem like that. I'm a simple country schoolteacher."

"It's five thousand pesos for the hour."

I pull on my trousers and place the damp banknotes the miller loaned me on the night table. She takes some water, wets the bangs on her forehead, and pats them smooth.

"I'm going back to Contulmo tonight. The train leaves in an hour."

"If you're in these parts again, I'll be here for you. My name's Rayén, but they call me Luna."

"Why?"

"Because I'm moony, because I always look at the moon, because I have a moon-shaped face. I don't know why. Everybody calls me Luna. What do they call you?"

"Prof."

"That's it?"

"That's it. Prof."

"Do you give good grades?"

"I've never flunked anybody."

"What grade would you give me in geography?"

She smiles and her teeth look as though they're about to jump out of her wide mouth.

"Russia?" I ask her.

"Moscow," she says, smiling even more broadly. "What grade?"

"An A."

"Are you serious? You'd give me an A in geography?"

"Absolutely. The highest grade."

"I can't wait to tell the other girls."

"All right."

She gives me her hand, quite formally. I grasp it, shake it, and slowly leave the whorehouse.

THIRTEEN

Outside the door they've still got a hitching post so cowboys can tie up their horses. The miller's standing there, yawning.

"So how was it?"

"Great."

"Good-looking chick?"

"Yes, Cristián, she was hot."

"What did you two talk about?"

"Foolishness. Ourselves. How about you?"

"We couldn't find a common theme. I mean, she wasn't a very communicative girl."

We take the dirt road to the train station. A slice of moon rises up amid black clouds. No rain, however. It's cold.

"So you and her didn't talk at all."

"Two or three words. Believe it or not, she asked me for a bread recipe."

"An interesting subject, Cristián. What's the recipe for baking a baguette?"

"The one your father used."

"What recipe did my father use?"

"You're putting me on. You want me to give you the recipe right now?"

"At this moment, there's nothing in the world I desire more than to know how to bake a baguette."

"Two kilos of flour, a cup and a half of warm water, one hundred grams of yeast, two and a half table-spoons of butter, three cups of water, a tablespoon of salt. All right?"

For a while I follow the moon's comings and goings in the ragged sky, and then I trip on a rock. I drop the little satchel I'm carrying, pick it up, and slap it against my thigh to knock off the dirt.

"If a person climbed up to the sails of the mill and jumped off, do you think he'd kill himself?"

"If anybody was crazy enough to do that, he'd probably break his neck."

FOURTEEN

The engineer's in his locomotive, resisting the cold with the aid of the brazier at his feet. An Araucan poncho covers his body. He holds out his thermos bottle to us and we drink coffee from the cap. He tells us we have a long wait, departure isn't until five o'clock. We'll arrive in Contulmo at seven.

He's got his day all planned. Breakfast at eight, Mass at nine, soccer at ten (Peleco versus Contulmo on Viera Gallo Field), lunch at one, the weekend soap opera on the radio at two, siesta at three, and then at four he has to drive the locomotive back to Angol.

He's afraid that Chilean State Railroads will close down this branch line because it has so few riders. And he's only three years from retirement. Except for the time when a heifer tried to cross the tracks, there's no major accident on his service record. On that occasion, he informed the owner of the ill-fated animal, who willingly turned it over to him for a big barbecue that was held the following day in Purén.

When the train finally leaves the station, there are eight passengers in our car. I'm shivering from my hair to my soles. The moon's gliding freely and swiftly through the sky. At least that's the illusion you have when you're traveling fast.

My teeth are all bashing one another. *Zazie dans le métro* falls off my lap. Cristián puts a hand on my forehead, and I can barely hear him when he says, "You're burning up with fever."

FIFTEEN

On Sunday I drink liters of warm lemonade and swallow aspirins every four hours, and Mama changes my sweaty sheets three times. Some boys from school stand under my window and call up to me that Contulmo won, one to nothing. We're leading the Malleco League. I want to read a bit of my novel, because I have the suspicion I'm going to need money very soon, and the only way for me to get some is to finish my translation. There are words I don't know, but when I look them up in my *Larousse,* my vision blurs.

My fever reveals something I may forget later. I write it down on a leaf of penmanship paper I find with the *Diary of My Life* I'm going to give Augusto Gutiérrez: "It's not the case that words circle uncertainly around subjects. It's the world itself that's uncertain; words are precise."

What will Gutiérrez's first journal entry be? I open the little window in my room and look out at the quiet sails of the mill. Cristián's asleep. The bread recipe. French baguette.

SIXTEEN

Monday goes past. According to my mother, I groaned like a woman giving birth and suddenly sat up wild-eyed on the bed. She gave me aspirin and lemonade, and at night a little chicken soup.

There are two pieces of correspondence for me. One, from Cristián, arrives in a yellowish envelope. Inside there's a note and a postcard.

The note reads,

> In regard to your father, I received the enclosed postcard from him today, sent from Paris. Also today, I was looking down at the ground from the top of the mill, and now I can give you a definite answer to your question. Anyone who jumped from up there would be smashed to pieces. It's not worth the trouble, especially if God has longer journeys in mind for us. The best conclusion is to live to be a great-grandfather and pass away in your bed, surrounded by your numerous family, after receiving extreme unction from the priest. Take the word of a lonely bachelor.

The postcard shows a painting of ballerinas doing bar exercises. On the back, the painter's name: Degas. Otherwise, emptiness and silence.

The second note comes from Gutiérrez:

Dear Prof,

Teresa's letter is in my hands. She seems to have copied the things she writes you from a book. She finds you quite distinguished, she's intoxicated by your gaze. She says that when you look at her, "Troy burns." I'm not sure what she means, but I gather that Tere will be very happy if you come to my party on Friday. The Chilean postal system is stupendous. As a birthday present, my uncle Mateo in Antofagasta sent me a cable transfer in the amount of 20,000 pesos. Next Saturday, rain or shine, I'm going to Angol. You're invited, Prof.

By six o'clock Tuesday morning, my fever has disappeared. I'm clearheaded, and I can distinguish every one of the birds and chickens that are warbling or clucking in the garden. I occupy my day off with *Zazie dans le métro.* I touch my growing bristles and decide not to peer into the mirror or shave. I'll show up at school tomorrow looking like a bandit. The kids will feel anxious, and they won't throw pieces of chalk at the blackboard when I turn my back on them.

For dinner, Mama brings me another dose of chicken broth, this time accompanied by two rolls.

"Cristián's gotten over his hangover," she remarks.

When she turns to go away, I take hold of her wrist and force her to sit on the edge of the bed. She looks at me with fright and curiosity but immediately starts feeling my sheets to make sure they've been properly dried and starched. She adheres in her own house to the norms of the hotel business.

"What do you know about Dad that I don't know, Mama?"

"He's in France."

"Why did he go away?"

"All men have a little sailor in them. Curiosity about other places. Besides, it's his native country, no?"

"What about me? What about you?"

She strokes her chin, and for an instant she looks like a ballerina. She's a shallow, distracted woman whose beauty is marked by melancholy. She says, "We're here, no?"

I spoon the soup with one hand and hold her wrist tight with the other so she won't go away. Then I start voraciously gobbling up the miller's bread. I'm as hungry as a wolf. The stubble on my chin lends me an unexpected audacity.

"Where's Pierre, Mama?"

"In Paris."

"And why?"

"He's from there. It's only natural."

"And when he left...didn't he love you anymore?"

"Why wouldn't he love me anymore? Of course he loved me. He loved you, too. But Paris..."

"Do you like movies, Mama?"

"I used to go to the theaters in Santiago a lot. In a few years, supposedly, television is going to come to Chile. Maybe by then we'll have enough money to buy a set."

I look at her as I've never done before. Without touching her, I strip the years from her, the effects of the daily grind. I see how lovely she is, how vulnerable. Youthful in the way older women are youthful.

Devastatingly attractive.

"Before you were born, your father would compare me with French and Italian actresses. There was one year when he called me Mylène Demongeot, another when I was Pier Angeli. Then I got old and he stopped giving me nicknames."

"You were prettier than those actresses."

"Are you going to hold classes tomorrow?"

"Of course, Mama. My fever's gone."

"You almost left with it, Jacques. I'll never let you go to Angol with Cristián again."

"I got sick because I didn't bring an overcoat."

"Acting like the young male lead in some movie."

"Yes, Mama. Never again."

I keep hold of her wrist. The exact words are there, but unfortunately they don't do their duty.

"What will you teach your young pupils tomorrow?"

"A little history. A bit of geography."

"What?"

"I'll talk to them about the tunnel on the road to Lonquimay."

"'Las Raíces?'"

"They've surely been through it several times, but they don't know it's 4,537 meters long. They don't know its construction required the removal of 184,000 cubic meters of rock with the help of 175,000 kilos of dynamite; they don't know that 240,000 bags of cement went into building the concrete tunnel lining."

Her eyes wide and unblinking, Mama hums a little tune to dissimulate the pride produced in her by the depth of my professional knowledge. I recognize Yves Montand's song "Je ferai le tour du monde."

"What time shall I serve you your breakfast?"

"Seven o'clock."

"In bed or at the table?"

"At the table."

SEVENTEEN

Throughout the rest of the week, my pupils behave like storybook children. They bring me apples, and before I eat them I rub them on the lapel of my jacket until they're shiny. To prevent Gutiérrez from asking me about Angol on my very first day back, I decide to give long dictations, which keep the pupils at their desks. I set them difficult words. For example, "disciplinary," "accession," "wallop."

EIGHTEEN

At noon on Wednesday, glancing through the window of the seamstress's workshop, I see Elena Gutiérrez, the older of Augusto Gutiérrez's sisters, trying on a blouse that needs to be taken in. Luckily, she's got her figure back, she says. In the South, she says, you eat so much cheese, and there's so much fat in the milk. Now she has only skinless chicken and vegetables for dinner and drinks a lot of parsley water.

She gets close to the mirror and says that her cheeks look "frightfully healthy." She'd like her cheekbones to be more prominent, she'd like to be as pale as Greta Garbo in *The Kiss.* She wants the blouse good and snug at the waist, she declares, and when a certain man puts his hand on her belt to lead her out to dance, she wants the embroidered hem of the blouse to feel good to him. She'd love it if the blouse could ride up a little when he pressed it and he could touch her skin.

I withdraw to the plaza before she can notice me and let one of my pupils, who works as a shoeshine boy, pass a cloth over Dad's former footwear. According to an announcement in the *Diario de Angol,* next month it will begin to publish Raymond Queneau's great novel *Zazie in the Metro.* The installments will run throughout the winter.

Two facts go unrevealed: I haven't turned in the book yet, and I haven't yet been paid the advance I was promised. Nor is the translator's name, my name, even mentioned.

I'd like to see my name in print sometime. A bit of fame would lend me prestige in Teresa's eyes. According to Gutiérrez, I have to ask her to dance, attach myself to her like a limpet, and breathe into her ear. I don't need to say anything to her. The girl's like the Electrola in the Danubio Azul, he informs me. She knows all the songs on the radio.

"You squeeze her and she'll sing. And then, Professor, I dim the lights, all at once, and you have to give her a French kiss."

I ask him why he's helping me so much in the conquest of his sister, and he says that one favor pays for another. He needs an adult to get him into the whorehouse in Angol, and I'm the only person in the world who can carry out that mission. Cleaning his spectacles on his shirttails, he says I'm his teacher and his friend. I'm the one who's taught him everything in life, from the triumph of the Chilean troops at the Battle of Yungay, where our hero General Manuel Bulnes thwarted the Bolivian Marshal Santa Cruz's efforts to unite Peru and Bolivia, to lessons in the best way to smoke a cigarette without coughing.

"Friday night will be yours, Professor Jacques, and Saturday night will belong to your disciple and servant Augusto Gutiérrez."

He asks me to feel the wad he's got in his pants pocket.

"That's the twenty thousand Uncle Mateo sent me—I carry it around so I won't lose it. The train for Angol leaves at four." Then, anticipating his moment of glory, he repeats himself. "Four o'clock Saturday," he says.

NINETEEN

On the day of the party, as if obeying a decree, almost all the men in the village put pomade in their hair. The weather's hazy, the temperature suddenly warm. Indian summer, as they say.

Gutiérrez is standing beside the phonograph, and after handing him his present I check out the labels on the 45s waiting to be loaded onto the cylinder: "Sincerely," by Lucho Gatica; Johnny Ray's "Walkin' in the Rain"; Paul Anka's "Diana"; Elvis Presley's "Heartbreak Hotel"; "Blue Tango," by Hugo Winterhalter and His Orchestra.

He pats me conspiratorially on the shoulder, and while he's opening the package I see Elena Gutiérrez, in her new embroidered blouse, refusing to let the hardware store owner light the cigarette she's holding in her lips. When the man insists, she blows out his match and wets the burned tip of the cigarette with saliva, all the while looking at me very meaningfully.

But then Teresa Gutiérrez comes up, she looks at me in her turn, and the two of them turn away laughing.

Augusto makes no effort to hide his disappointment in my offering. "A notebook with a padlock," he mumbles without enthusiasm.

"You can write personal things in it."

"What things?"

"The things that happen to you."

"Nothing happens to me, Prof."

"But something may start happening to you very soon, and it would be a shame not to record it."

"For example?"

"The trip to Angol. I'd like to know everything you do, in detail."

He offers me the palm of his hand with his raised fingers spread so we can exchange a knowing high five. Elena Gutiérrez appears, carrying a glass. She plants it in my right hand and remains cheekily at my side. Frankie Laine is singing "Jezebel" on the record player.

"Cuba libre," she tells me. "With Jamaican rum."

"It's better than Mitjans."

"Do you want to dance?"

I glimpse her sister Teresa, whose eyes are fixed on me as she sips Coca-Cola through a straw.

"Actually, I thought I'd dance the slow songs with Teresa."

"'Jezebel' isn't all that slow. It's half foxtrot and half tango. Let's dance."

I leave the glass on the table next to the phonograph and put my hand on her waist, on her highly polished belt. She reacts to my fingers and my steps with impeccable docility. Holding her straw wedged between her upper incisors and drumming her fingers on the empty bottle, Teresa watches us dance.

Gutiérrez turns off the ceiling light, leaving two dim bulbs burning in the corners of the living room. We're about a dozen people in all, and except for Gutiérrez, everyone's dancing.

Out of the corner of my eye, I see him go over to the buffet and add one more candle to the fifteen his father has already stuck into the frosting of the birthday cake.

Elena raises my hand, which she's holding at shoulder level, and places it over her heart. "I've had my eye on you for some time, Jacques," she says.

"To laugh at me."

"I laughed to hide myself."

"What does that mean?"

"You and I have something in common. A secret."

"I have no idea what secret that could be."

"If I say a name to you, do you promise to keep quiet?"

I notice that her hand is making mine sweat profusely. I try to pull away from her so I can wipe it on my lapel, but she doesn't let me go. On the contrary, she presses my hand against her with great urgency.

"You can trust me," I say.

"Good."

She raises her solemn eyes, and although she says the name in the tone of a secret, she can't help thrusting out her chin with a hint of pride: "Emilio."

She waits precisely three seconds before thrusting the blade in all the way: "Emilio," she repeats. "Like Émile Zola."

The phonograph needle falls on "Love Is a Many-Splendored Thing," by the Four Aces. I dig my fingers into the embroidery on the hem of her blouse.

The ice in my glass has melted already, and I can't bring myself to pick it up. I don't swallow the saliva pooling in my throat. I look at the other couples' feet. The girls are wearing high heels; the boys have slathered polish on their shoes. The Gutiérrez siblings' father is standing on the threshold, stretching his suspenders with his thumbs out past the front of his open jacket.

I move away from Elena, open a door, and step out into the rear patio. The house dog barks at me, but I ignore it. Elena has followed me outside.

"You and I had to talk, Jacques. I'm sorry if I hurt you."

"It's all right."

"This is a very small village, and the secret we've kept for two years is very big. Letting it out wouldn't be in anybody's interest. That was why I left the village for a year."

"Who else knows?"

"The miller."

"Why did he let me go off on my own in Angol? Didn't it occur to him that I might run into my father?"

"He's a drunk, as you know. But he's also a wise man."

"What makes you say that?"

"He took you to the whorehouse so you'd forget about my sister."

"What does one of those things have to do with the other?"

The girl goes over to a faucet, turns it on, and lets the water run over her forehead. Then she pats her neck with her wet hands. It's dark, and the only light is coming from the dog's little house.

"There are two kegs of dynamite in this village, Jacques. If someone accidentally drops a lighted match, the whole place could explode."

"And?"

"I don't want what happened to me with your father to happen to my sister."

"Why didn't you keep Emilio?"

"This is Augusto's birthday party. It's not the place to discuss such things."

"I'm not the one who started it."

"Of course you started it! You started it with your stupid trip to Angol! I want to be the star of my own life, not a slave to a child."

"You don't love him, then."

"Your father loved you, and nevertheless he left you. You're a schoolteacher, Jacques! You ought to know that many things in life are very complex."

"They're simpler than you imagine. My father loved me and left me. My father loves Emilio and doesn't leave him. I'm an abandoned dog, Elena."

"All you have to do is bark," she says with a smile.

She pulls the thin chain out of her cleavage and places the little golden cross between her teeth.

"Do you see him sometimes?"

"No."

"I mean my father."

"Him neither. Nothing ever happened here, Jacques. And then, all of a sudden, something was growing between us. It was nice to have a secret in the village. You didn't know it, my dad didn't know it, your mother didn't know it. But reality destroyed everything. I was the heroine of a great movie, and your father was my leading man. A movie for just the two of us. We were the actors and the audience at the same time."

"The leading man in your movie is now projecting films in the Angol cinema. He's in the projection booth for the matinees, the double features, the evening showings. He's not going to win an Oscar like that."

"Don't think I don't have feelings. Sometimes I think sad thoughts about Emilio."

"And who knows, maybe sometimes my father thinks sad thoughts about me," I say, swallowing at last.

The lights go out.

"They're going to light the candles and sing 'Happy Birthday,'" she says.

"Augusto put sixteen candles on his cake. Someone ought to help him blow them out."

The girl removes the little cross from her mouth and lays it across my lips. She says, "Swear you'll keep quiet."

TWENTY

In the living room, Augusto Gutiérrez has opened the present from his father and is now wearing it as he glides around the room, dancing to "Blue Tango" with an imaginary partner and flicking a flashlight on and off to illuminate his new jacket. He's going for the dance hall effect. The jacket's a Windbreaker, the same color and style as the one James Dean wears in *Rebel Without a Cause.*

We gather around the table, and the father does me the honor of handing me the knife and indicating that I should cut the cake as soon as the candles are blown out. As he's doing this, he spots the additional candle, plucks it out of the cake, and throws it on a plate.

He's a heavyset, dark-complexioned man whose corpulence has softened his Indian cheekbones. His enormous basketball player's hands give us the sign to begin the song.

The elder Gutiérrez's eyes shine with intense happiness: he's been a good widower, his daughters are lovely, and some day distinguished suitors from the outside world will come courting and marry them. Furthermore, the youngest of his children is friends with the schoolteacher, which guarantees him good grades and an academic future. Maybe he'll become a teacher, too.

Instead of cramming my mouth with the creamy piece of cake Augusto offers me, I put more ice in my Cuba libre and head for the bathroom, forcefully sipping the drink as I walk along.

In the hall, just as I'm about to open the door of the bathroom, I run into Teresa.

"Do you want to go first?" she asks me.

"I'm not in a hurry. Go ahead."

I notice that she's short of breath and unsteady on her feet.

"I just want to throw some water on my face. It's hot in here."

"This Cuba libre's ice-cold. Want some?"

She accepts but doesn't drink. Instead she raises the glass and rolls it over her burning cheeks.

"What relief!" she exclaims, closing her eyes and abandoning herself to the coolness of the glass.

I move closer to her to recover my drink, and when I see her damp cheeks so close, I feel as though my lips were pressed against that skin.

Then she says, "Excuse me."

She goes into the bathroom and closes the door. I hear her slide the bolt.

I remain right outside, like someone waiting his turn.

Her father appears in the hall and greets me merrily.

I raise one thumb. Everything's OK.

Since I'm standing so close to the door, I can clearly hear Teresa open the latch. I step back so she'll have room to pass.

But the girl doesn't come out.

Audacity accelerates the throbbing of that vein in my neck. Absurdly enough, I touch the knot in my tie and make sure it's properly centered.

I open the door. At first, I can make out only shapes. We're practically in the dark. I close the door behind me, and this time I'm the one who slides the bolt. Teresa's leaning on the washbasin and breathing hard. Perry Como's singing "Magic Moments" on the record player outside. I move toward her, seize one of the buttons on her blouse like a professional, and deliberately take a minute to undo it.

I remember the image Elena used: "Here in this village, there are two kegs of dynamite." The fuse is in my hands, at the end of my tongue.

I pucker her lips with my fingers and elect to kiss her for the first time like that. When I move away, she's undone the second button of her blouse, and now I can make out her brassiere hanging from the washbasin. She exposes her breasts demurely and without emphasis. She's trying to act natural, but she's trembling.

"I wrote you a letter, Jacques."

"I never got it."

"That's because I never sent it."

"Why not?"

"A letter leaves a trail. And what I told you was very serious."

I put one hand low on her stomach, and while she caresses my hair, I softly bite her chin.

"Tell me."

"I want to be with you, but not here."

"It's the only place where we can lock ourselves in."

"But it's my house, Jacques. I don't want to do it with you in this jail."

"Cristián could let us use his room."

"The mill's full of rats and cockroaches."

She's so wet that it comes through her skirt. When I move my hand away, in spite of the darkness we can both see the stain.

"I have to go and change," she says.

She throws the brassiere in the bathtub, buttons her

top button, opens the bolt, and quickly steps out into the hall.

The light from outside allows me to get a good look at myself in the mirror. I move closer to it, drawn by something strange in my expression.

"J'ai vieilli!"

The French of my childhood has returned, clouding the glass with my breath. I remember the character in *Zazie dans le métro* and what she says at the end of the novel when asked what she did in Paris.

"J'ai vieilli," she says.

"I got old," I repeat.

As I say those words, I make some decisions.

TWENTY-ONE

Decisions.

Like a feverish architect, I sketch out what I'm going to do this Saturday while the dawn rain washes away the accumulated dirt on the windows.

The day's agenda goes like this:

One, make an agenda
Two, visit Cristián
Three, have breakfast with Mama and persuade her, one way or another
Four, money Gutiérrez
Five, agreement Gutiérrez, precise instructions, i.e., train
Six, Teresa
Seven, conclusions (should there be any)

In the mill I find Cristián, perfectly shaven, wearing a tall, immaculate chef's hat and a fashionable linen jacket that nearly makes him look like a yacht skipper. Today he's not using his regular apron, the one that's dusty with flour and decorated with red wine stains.

"I didn't bake any bread last Saturday, and my customers are furious. They're afraid I'm not going to deliver the goods, so they're coming here to get it in person. I bought this outfit in Angol. You like it?"

"Did you find it in the same store as the Degas postcard with the ballerinas?"

Cristián reddens and slips six *marraquetas,* hot from the oven, into my jute tote bag. The loaves are wrapped in a sky-blue cloth with red Chilean bellflowers embroidered in its corners.

"The money for the girl last Saturday was a loan. You owe me, Jacques."

"I'll pay you as soon as I get the fee for my translations."

"All right."

TWENTY-TWO

Today I got up before my mother did. I put ground coffee in the cloth filter and dripped boiling water over it. The milk is heating on the stove as I cut two pieces of buttery *mantecoso* cheese, still fresh inside its waxed-paper wrapping. I turn an empty marmalade jar into a flower vase, fill it with water, and balance a single daisy in it as best I can.

Mama comes in to fix breakfast and is surprised to find everything ready. She's washed her hair in the shower and wrapped it in a blue towel. A scent of lavender floats around her. She puts sugar in her coffee and milk, stirs it with a teaspoon, and looks at me distrustfully. I've got my elbows on the tablecloth and my chin in the palms of my hands.

"What is it we have to discuss?"

"Your life, Mama dear."

"We're going to talk about my life?"

"Yes. About how you feel, about what you need."

"I feel fine, and I don't need anything."

"But you never go out. Your hands are all pale from washing so many sheets and tablecloths."

"There's not much to see in Contulmo."

"But you could go somewhere out of the village. Angol, for instance."

"And come back with a fever like you?"

"You have your fur coat."

"It's much too luxurious to wear in such backwaters."

She delicately chews one of the miller's little loaves with a slice of cheese and soundlessly sips her coffee and milk. I put my hand in my shirt pocket and hand her the envelope.

"What's this?"

"A free ticket to the movie they're showing tonight."

"You're crazy. Me, go to a movie?"

"You always used to go to the movies in Santiago. You'd tell me the stories of everything you saw. Now you're always silent. It's like something has eaten your tongue and your heart."

"Two hours on the train to see a movie?"

Now I take my ticket for Angol out of my pants pocket.

"Jacques?"

"Mami?"

"The fever."

"What about it?"

"I think it did you some damage."

She looks at the movie ticket in one hand and the train ticket in the other. With a jerk she undoes the knot in the towel holding her hair, and the lavender scent permeates the kitchen magnificently. I drink my coffee and smile approvingly at her.

"You're hiding something from me, Jacques."

"Yes."

"What is it?"

"I'd rather not tell you."

"If you don't tell me, I'm not going to the movie theater."

I chew my sandwich, not taking my eyes off her. It's difficult to make deals with Mama. For example, if I tell her what I intend to tell her, that doesn't mean she'll automatically go to the theater.

"I need to be alone in the house tonight."

"The miller says you want to commit suicide."

"He's a blabbermouth."

"If you commit suicide, I'll kill you," she says with a smile.

She runs a finger over my lips as though sealing a promise.

"Actually, Mama, the truth is there's this girl."

"From the village?"

"Mm-hmm."

"Do I know her?"

"I don't believe there's anyone in this burg you don't know."

"Is she pretty?"

"Indeed."

"Teresa Gutiérrez!"

"Yes, Teresa Gutiérrez, Mama."

"She's going to sleep with you?"

We sip our coffee for a while without saying anything. Inside the church, the priest rings the bell, the first of seven strokes.

"I don't know, Mama. You can't predict these things."

"What's the Saturday afternoon film? Some western?"

"No western this week. They're showing a movie with Anna Magnani and Anthony Quinn."

"What's it about?"

"I read the summary in *Screen*. It's set in some remote part of the United States. He's a widower, and she's come to replace his dead wife. But then he spends all his time comparing this new wife with the deceased one. And then she falls in love with a young man—"

"Where am I going to sleep in Angol?"

The sun is slowly spreading over the rustic tablecloth. When the rays reach the breadbasket, Mama lifts the cloth that's covering the little loaves and exposes them to the sunlight.

I press my eyelids together hard, a way I have of controlling my nerves. I take a loaf of bread and break it apart to no purpose. I don't want to eat anymore.

"God will provide," I say slowly.

In truth, I'm *praying* slowly.

TWENTY-THREE

At ten in the morning, I've got an appointment with Augusto Gutiérrez on the school basketball court. He shows up with his galactic eyeglasses, wearing short jeans and sneakers.

I pass him the ball and watch as he makes a basket on his first shot.

I figure this is his lucky day.

We sit on a tree stump next to the little bleachers, and I accept the Richmond cigarette he offers me with a grown-up's aplomb.

"Have you brought what I asked you to?"

He takes the banknotes out of his pocket, twenty thousand pesos held together by a yellow rubber band. I extract three bills and stuff them in my pants.

I've got the ball under my left foot and I'm moving it around. I say, "This is a loan, you understand me? When I get paid for *Zazie in the Metro,* I'll pay you back."

"That's fine, Prof."

"How do you feel?"

"Terrible. I turned fifteen and nothing happened."

"Your problem is you think only about your virginity. You have to arrive at sex in a more subtle way."

"Prof, if you called me here to give me a lesson, let me remind you that today is Saturday and there's no school!"

He kicks the ball out from under my foot and tears off down the court, dribbling the ball around imaginary opponents like a soccer player. He stops under the basket at the other end, kicks the ball straight up, catches it in his hands, and scores again.

He comes back to me in an excellent mood.

"The money you loaned me," I say. "It was for this."

I take out a train ticket and lay it across his bare knees.

"Are we going to Angol?"

"You're going to Angol."

"By myself?"

"You've been crowing about being fifteen years old."

"They won't let me in, Prof."

"How do you know?"

"I tried two years ago."

"Ah, you were a baby then."

He scratches the area between his nose and his lips and then asks me to feel it.

"Can't you tell? I'm starting a mustache."

The plan I made at dawn is being carried out precisely. I hand him an envelope with a card inside containing instructions for the next steps he's to take.

"Open it at home, and be at the train station at four o'clock."

"Will do, Prof."

"Make sure you bring every item on the list I just gave you."

"Of course."

"You won't need more than five thousand pesos. There's no reason for you to go there with that whole roll of bills in your pocket."

"Five thousand. Got it."

"And put on long pants and a tie. You're going to see a lady."

Gutiérrez touches his throat as if the red tie were already knotted around his neck.

"Five thousand pesos, *Diary of My Life,* long pants," he enumerates.

"The rest of the money stays home."

"You're a great teacher, Prof."

"You can mention that to the judge in the local police court when the time comes. I could wind up in jail for this."

Augusto Gutiérrez looks anxiously at his watch and snaps his fingers, encouraging the hands to advance without pause to four in the afternoon.

TWENTY-FOUR

At three fifty-five in the afternoon, the normally empty platform in the Contulmo train station looks like the scene of a political gathering.

There are three clearly distinct groups.

My mother is wrapped in her fur coat, sporting a felt hat like something out of a forties movie, black kid gloves, and an umbrella, which she dangles pensively.

Teresa Gutiérrez is wearing a skirt and a man's jacket, with a gray scarf covering her shoulders and her neck and, at her feet, a leather suitcase the color of pale coffee.

The stationmaster is trying to tie the various ends together, maybe even inventing a story for all these characters.

And now there's me.

Bleeding as though from a bullet wound, but obsessed with my plot.

Before approaching my protagonists, I head for the stationmaster. I want to instruct him as to what he must say when Augusto Gutiérrez's dad crosses the tracks in his pajamas later tonight, waving a flashlight and looking for his children Augusto and Teresa. The stationmaster must lie and tell Teresa's father that he saw the two of them leave for Angol together.

"A lot of movement today," I say.

"A wide range. Including your *señora madre,* right?"

"Yes. She's going to Angol to pick up a package my father sent her from Paris."

"And the Gutiérrez kids."

"Teresa's accompanying Augusto to the store to exchange a birthday present that's too small for him. A Windbreaker like James Dean's."

"And you?" he asks me.

"I'm here to tell Mama good-bye."

Next I go over to the Gutiérrez group.

Teresa is pale and vacant. The remnant of childhood that once protected her seems to have melted away. She stands before me, desperately available. I've made up this farce of her traveling to Angol so that I can remove her clothes as I like, in my own bed. Here in Contulmo.

Now I examine my student. The gray pants are perfect, the blue jacket well ironed, the red tie with the white spots very cheerful, the hair, subdued by some implacable gel, very adult.

And in the midst of all, triumphant as a blue apple, the globe that helped him get the school's highest grade in geography.

"You're to give that to Señorita Luna."

"The world and the five thousand pesos?"

"First the world, and then, if the occasion should arise, the five thousand pesos."

Getting him to take her the globe as a gift was my idea.

The train pulls into the station, needlessly whistling. Today only dogs are crossing the tracks.

Sometimes I think the engineer blows that whistle just to keep himself from falling asleep. As calm and steady and experienced as this train is, it could get to Angol even without a driver.

I go over to Mama and help her up the steps and into the car. She stoops to kiss me on the forehead.

"Have a good time, Jacques."

"You too, Mami."

"Tell me about it tomorrow."

"We'll tell each other tomorrow."

"What's the name of the movie with Anna Magnani?"

"Wild Is the Wind."

The stationmaster blows his little whistle and checks his wristwatch for the tenth time to be sure it's four p.m. and reflects upon the fact that the platform clock has been stopped at ten minutes after three for five years.

TWENTY-FIVE

Back home, I barely have time to take the pitcher of lemonade out of the refrigerator and pour Teresa a glass before she starts to cry. I'd like to ask her what's wrong and console her. Smell her skin and stroke her earlobes. Lick her eyelids and swallow her youthful mascara as it dissolves on my tongue.

But my heart's elsewhere.

Its grave throbbing accompanies the heavy wheels of the train bound for the movie theater in Angol.

Emilio needs a mother to take care of him.

ANTONIO SKÁRMETA is a Chilean author who wrote the novel that inspired the 1994 Academy Award-winning movie *Il Postino: The Postman*. His fiction has received dozens of awards and has been translated into nearly thirty languages. In 2011 his novel *The Days of the Rainbow* won the prestigious Premio Iberoamericano Planeta-Casa de América de Narrativa. His play *El Plebiscito*, based on the same true event, was the basis for the Oscar-nominated film *No*.

JOHN CULLEN is the translator of many books from Spanish, French, German, and Italian, including Yasmina Khadra's Middle East Trilogy (*The Swallows of Kabul*, *The Attack*, and *The Sirens of Baghdad*), Eduardo Sacheri's *The Secret in Their Eyes*, Carlos Zanón's *The Barcelona Brothers*, and Rithy Panh's *The Elimination*. He lives in upstate New York.

PUBLISHER'S NOTE

This is a work of fiction. Names, characters, places, and incidents either are the product of the author's imagination or are used fictitiously, and any resemblance to actual persons, living or dead, events, or locales is entirely coincidental.